My Dad, the Rock-and-Roll Penguin

Written by Matthew Dunstan
Illustrated by Fraser Williamson

W9-CFW-677

Contents

Not So Loud, Dad

My family is a family of soft-music penguins. Everyone likes soft music. Everyone, that is, except my dad. My dad is not a soft-music penguin. He's a rock-and-roll penguin.

One day his rock-and-roll music started an avalanche! All the snow and ice on the ice cliffs broke loose and crashed down. Luckily no one was hurt.

But there was a very big fuss and the Penguin Council made Dad leave the penguin colony. I was very sad because I missed my dad.

Gentle Music on Ice

Every year my mother, my grandmother, and I give a music concert to all our friends. All the seals, the sea lions, and the penguins come.

Last year, we held the concert on the ice. The concert was called *Gentle Music on Ice*.

My mother, Penelope Penguin, played the harp and my grandmother rang the icicle bells.

I played the piano. I've been learning the piano since I was a very little penguin.

The music we made was soft and gentle.
The seals, the sea lions, and the penguins
seemed to be enjoying themselves.

Then Dad arrived. He jumped up onto the stage and started singing,

I am a rock-and-roll penguin,
I am cool, I am fast.
I am from the future,
Not from the past!

It was not a soft-music concert any more!
It was a loud rock-and-roll concert! My
mother was really angry when Dad tried
to play her harp. So that was the end of
that concert.

Sweet Sounds on Ice

Dad told me that he wouldn't play his loud music at our next concert. My mother, my grandmother, and I were going to have the concert on one of the icebergs. This concert was called *Sweet Sounds on Ice*.

For the first time, the Penguin Council invited the orcas to come to the concert. The orcas said that they had wanted to come to one of our soft-music concerts for a long time. They said that they were big fans of our soft music. But the orcas really hated rock-and-roll music. It hurt their ears.

When Dad heard that the orcas were coming to the concert, he said to me,

"Be careful, Percy. Orcas are also called killer whales. You can't trust them if they don't like rock-and-roll."

"I'll be careful," I said. "But please, Dad, don't come and play loud music again. You'll never be allowed back into the penguin colony if you don't start playing soft rock-and-roll music!"

"Don't worry, Percy, I'll stay away from the stage this time," Dad said. "I'll be watching those orcas from Snowy Ridge."

It was a beautiful concert. Our music was soft and gentle. Icebergs floated past like silent mountains.

The seals and the sea lions clapped and barked. The orcas swam round in pretty patterns in time to the icicle bells.

Then I heard that sound! It was Dad! He was zooming along Snowy Ridge, where he had been watching the orcas. I could see him. He was wearing his bright red shirt.

Everyone was watching Dad come closer. No one was listening to our soft music now. The penguins all waved their flippers at Dad. They were trying to make him slow down.

Then the ice shook! My piano tipped off the iceberg and fell into the sea.

What had happened? Just then the orcas broke the ice bridge that joined us to the shore! The seals, the sea lions, and the penguins were trapped on the iceberg. The orcas had tricked us!

Dad Saves the Day

Dad was moving very fast. He jumped over the water onto our iceberg. Just in time! An orca was trying to bite me! Whack! Dad hit the orca on the nose.

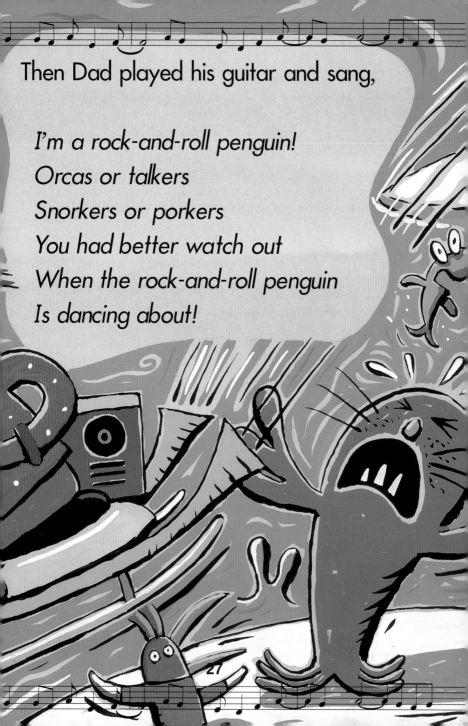

Then Dad played his guitar and sang,

I'm a rock-and-roll penguin!
Orcas or talkers
Snorkers or porkers
You had better watch out
When the rock-and-roll penguin
Is dancing about!

Dad sang very loud. The music was too loud for the orcas, so they plunged under the water and banged their big heads against the iceberg again. The ice shook. The orcas were trying to knock us off the iceberg!

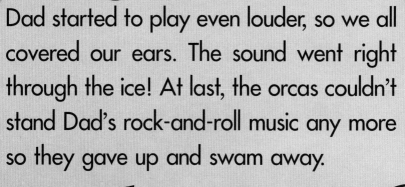

Dad started to play even louder, so we all covered our ears. The sound went right through the ice! At last, the orcas couldn't stand Dad's rock-and-roll music any more so they gave up and swam away.

Then Dad got a rope and an ice hook. He threw the ice hook onto the shore.

Dad was a hero, so he was elected to the Penguin Council. Now, I'm learning to play the drums and, next year, we're going to have a rock-and-roll concert.